nickelodeon

降圭神通

AVATAR
THE LAST AIRBENDER

ISBN 978-0-593-43124-5

rhcbooks.com

Printed in the United States of America
10 9 8 7 6 5 4 3 2 1

nickelodeon

降击神通

AVATAR

THE LAST AIRBENDER

ZUKO FINDS HIS WAY

Random House • New York

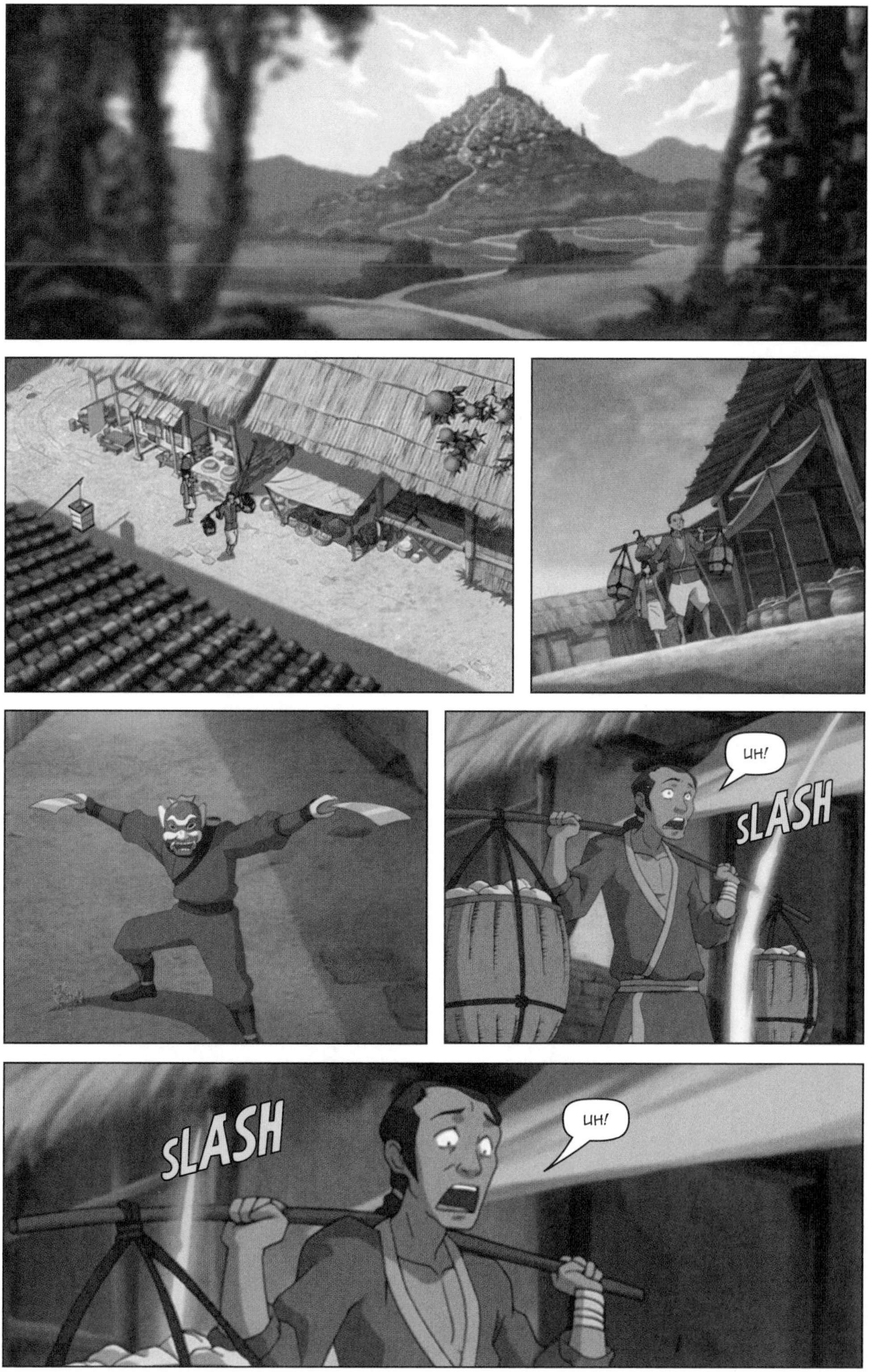
UH!
SLASH
SLASH
UH!

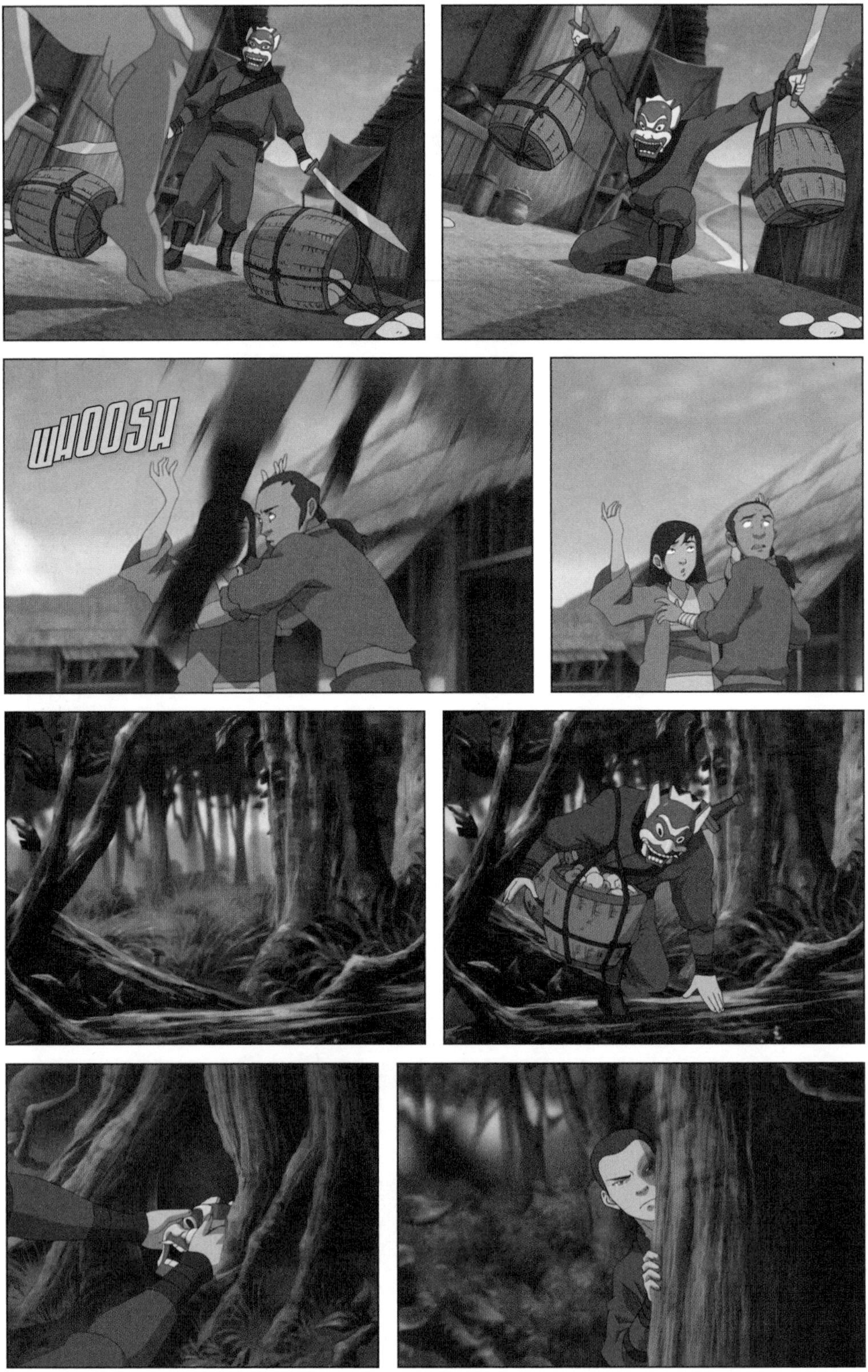
WHOOSH

WHERE DID YOU GET THESE?

WHAT DOES IT MATTER WHERE THEY CAME FROM?

HMM...

MMM!

A FEW DAYS LATER...

WHAM

GRUNT

4

WHEW!

SMASH

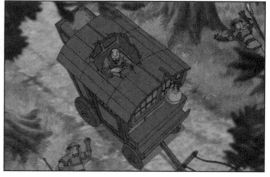

THAT NIGHT...

LOOKS LIKE YOU DID SOME SERIOUS SHOPPING. BUT WHERE DID YOU GET THE MONEY?

DO YOU LIKE YOUR NEW TEAPOT?

TO BE HONEST WITH YOU, THE BEST TEA TASTES DELICIOUS WHETHER IT COMES IN A PORCELAIN POT OR A TIN CUP.

I KNOW WE'VE HAD SOME DIFFICULT TIMES LATELY. WE'VE HAD TO STRUGGLE JUST TO GET BY.

BUT IT'S NOTHING TO BE ASHAMED OF. THERE IS A SIMPLE HONOR IN POVERTY.

THERE'S NO HONOR FOR ME WITHOUT THE AVATAR.

ZUKO...EVEN IF YOU DID CAPTURE THE AVATAR, I'M NOT SO SURE IT WOULD SOLVE OUR PROBLEMS. NOT NOW.

NO, ZUKO! YOU MUST NEVER GIVE IN TO DESPAIR.

ALLOW YOURSELF TO SLIP DOWN THAT ROAD AND YOU SURRENDER TO YOUR LOWEST INSTINCTS.

THEN THERE IS NO HOPE AT ALL.

IN THE DARKEST TIMES, HOPE IS SOMETHING YOU GIVE YOURSELF.

THAT IS THE MEANING OF INNER STRENGTH.

LATER...

UNCLE...

I THOUGHT A LOT ABOUT WHAT YOU SAID.

YOU DID? GOOD, GOOD.

IT'S HELPED ME REALIZE SOMETHING.

WE NO LONGER HAVE ANYTHING TO GAIN BY TRAVELING TOGETHER.

I NEED TO FIND MY OWN WAY.

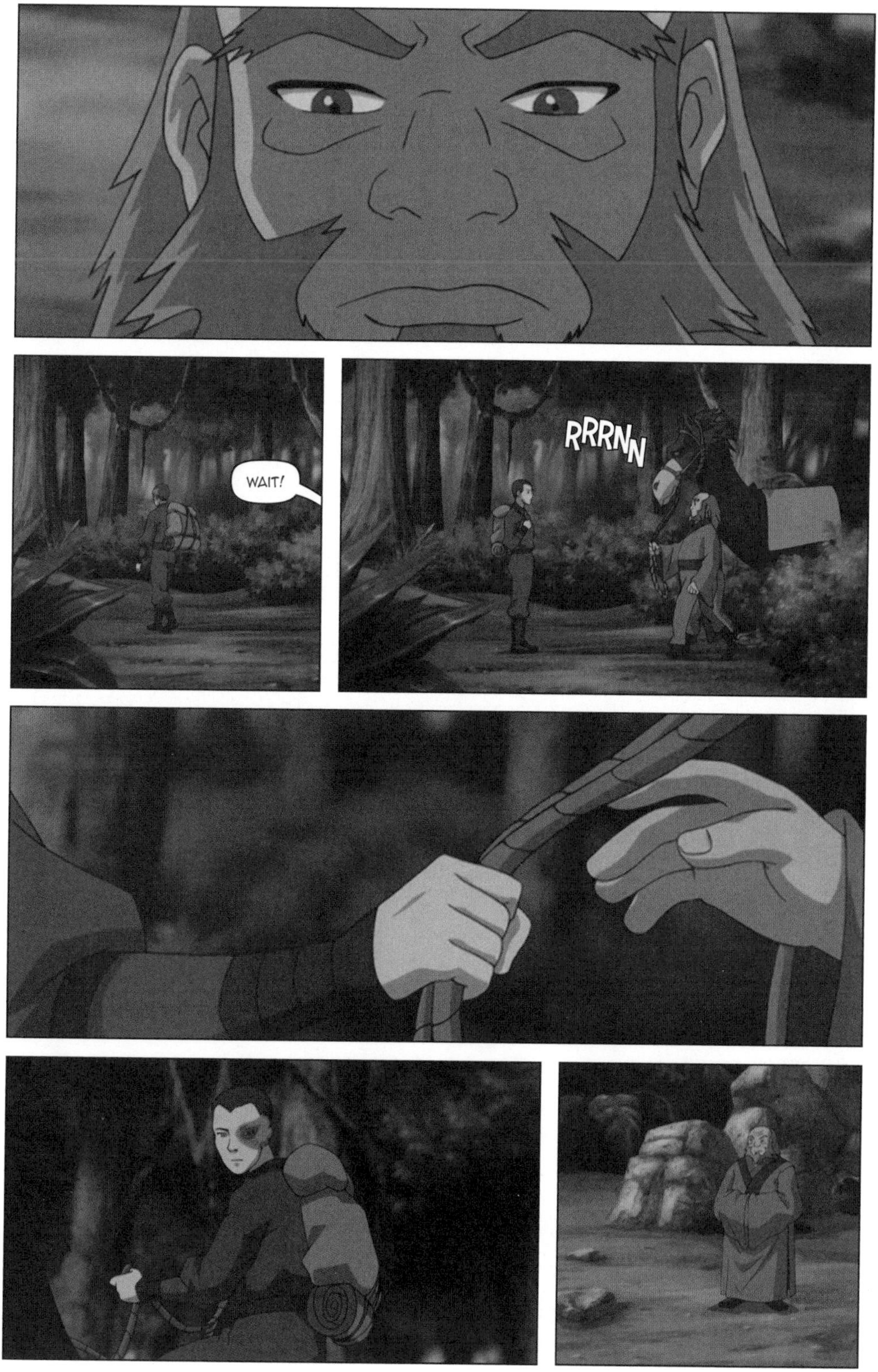
WAIT!
RRRNN

MANY DAYS LATER, NEAR A SMALL EARTH KINGDOM VILLAGE...

COME ON,
SPIDER-SNAKE
EYES.

HAHA!
YEAH!

COULD I GET SOME WATER, A BAG OF FEED, AND SOMETHING HOT TO EAT?

NOT ENOUGH HERE FOR A HOT MEAL.

I CAN GET YOU TWO BAGS OF FEED.

HEHEHE!

HA!

SPLAT

OW!

HEY! YOU THROWING EGGS AT US, STRANGER?

NO.

YOU SEE WHO DID THROW IT?

NO.

IT HAD TO COME FROM SOMEWHERE.

THAT YOUR FAVORITE WORD, "NO"?

MAYBE A CHICKEN FLEW OVER.

THANKS FOR YOUR CONTRIBUTION. THE ARMY APPRECIATES YOUR SUPPORT.

YOU BETTER LEAVE TOWN. PENALTY FOR STAYING'S A LOT STEEPER THAN YOU CAN AFFORD, STRANGER.

TRUST ME.

THANKS FOR NOT RATTING ME OUT.

THOSE SOLDIERS ARE SUPPOSED TO PROTECT US FROM THE FIRE NATION. BUT THEY'RE JUST A BUNCH OF THUGS.

I'LL TAKE YOU TO MY HOUSE AND FEED YOUR OSTRICH HORSE FOR YOU. COME ON, I OWE YOU.

OINK

BAA BAA

OINK

NO ONE CAN EVER SNEAK UP ON US.

NO KIDDING.

YOU A FRIEND OF LEE'S?

THIS GUY JUST STOOD UP TO THE SOLDIERS. BY THE END, HE PRACTICALLY HAD THEM RUNNING AWAY.

DOES THIS GUY HAVE A NAME?

I'M, UH...

HE DOESN'T HAVE TO SAY WHO HE IS IF HE DOESN'T WANT TO, SELA.

ANYONE WHO CAN HOLD HIS OWN AGAINST THOSE BULLY SOLDIERS IS WELCOME HERE. THOSE MEN SHOULD BE ASHAMED TO WEAR EARTH KINGDOM UNIFORMS.

THE REAL SOLDIERS ARE OFF FIGHTING THE WAR. LIKE LEE'S BIG BROTHER, SENSU.

SUPPER'S GOING TO BE READY SOON. WOULD YOU LIKE TO STAY?

I CAN'T...I SHOULD BE MOVING ON.

GANSU COULD USE SOME HELP ON THE BARN. WHY DON'T YOU TWO WORK FOR A WHILE, AND THEN WE'LL EAT?

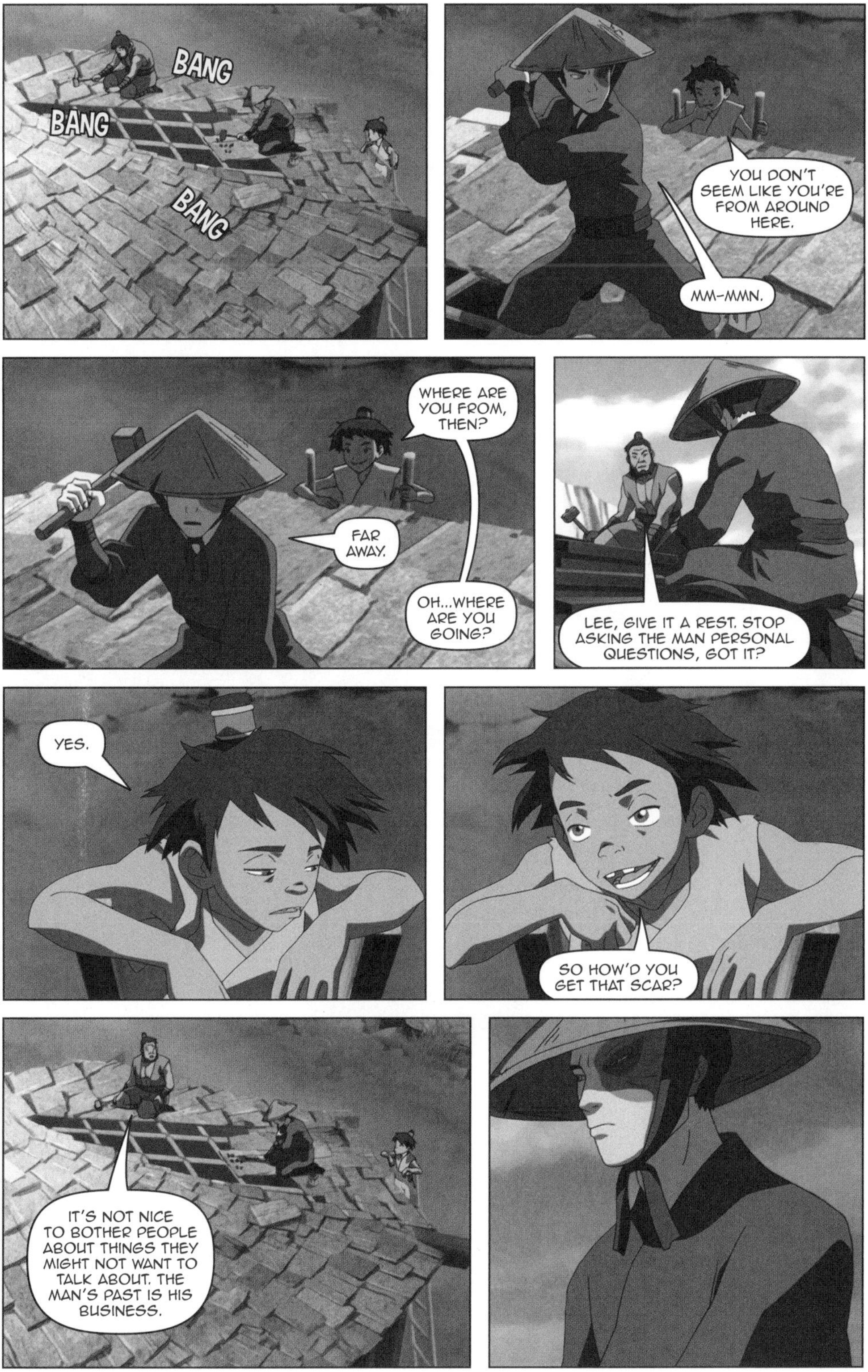
BANG
BANG
BANG
YOU DON'T SEEM LIKE YOU'RE FROM AROUND HERE.
MM-MMN.
WHERE ARE YOU FROM, THEN?
FAR AWAY.
OH...WHERE ARE YOU GOING?
LEE, GIVE IT A REST. STOP ASKING THE MAN PERSONAL QUESTIONS, GOT IT?
YES.
SO HOW'D YOU GET THAT SCAR?
IT'S NOT NICE TO BOTHER PEOPLE ABOUT THINGS THEY MIGHT NOT WANT TO TALK ABOUT. THE MAN'S PAST IS HIS BUSINESS.

HEY, MOM, WANT TO SEE HOW AZULA FEEDS TURTLE DUCKS?

SQUAWK

ZUKO, WHY WOULD YOU DO THAT?

SQUAWK

CHOMP

OW, OW–OW!

OW!

STUPID TURTLE DUCK. WHY'D SHE DO THAT?

ZUKO, THAT'S WHAT MOMS ARE LIKE.

IF YOU MESS WITH THEIR BABIES, HRUM! THEY'RE GONNA BITE YOU BACK.

HAHAHA.

19

WATCH THIS.

TEE-HEE

MOM, CAN YOU MAKE ZUKO PLAY WITH US? WE NEED EQUAL TEAMS TO PLAY A GAME.

I AM NOT CARTWHEELING.

YOU WON'T HAVE TO. CARTWHEELING'S NOT A GAME, DUM-DUM.

I DON'T CARE. I DON'T WANT TO PLAY WITH YOU.

WE ARE BROTHER AND SISTER. IT'S IMPORTANT FOR US TO SPEND TIME TOGETHER.

DON'T YOU THINK SO, MOM?

YES, DARLING, I THINK IT'S A GOOD IDEA TO PLAY WITH YOUR SISTER. GO ON, NOW, JUST FOR A LITTLE WHILE.

HERE'S THE WAY IT GOES. NOW WHAT YOU DO IS TRY TO KNOCK THE APPLE OFF THE OTHER PERSON'S HEAD, LIKE THIS.

FWOOSH

FOOM

AAAHHH!

SPLASH

SEE, I TOLD YOU IT WOULD WORK.

AW, THEY'RE SO CUTE TOGETHER.

YOU TWO ARE SUCH... UGH!

I WAS JUST COMING TO GET YOU. UNCLE IROH SENT US A LETTER FROM THE WAR FRONT.

YOU'RE SOAKING WET.

GIRLS ARE CRAZY!

22

"IF THE CITY IS AS MAGNIFICENT AS ITS WALL, BA SING SE MUST BE SOMETHING TO BEHOLD.

"I HOPE YOU ALL MAY SEE IT SOMEDAY. IF WE DON'T BURN IT TO THE GROUND FIRST. HEHE."

HA-HA!

"UNTIL THEN, ENJOY THESE GIFTS."

HA-HA!

"FOR ZUKO, A PEARL DAGGER..."

"...FROM THE GENERAL WHO SURRENDERED WHEN WE BROKE THROUGH THE OUTER WALL.

"NOTE THE INSCRIPTION AND THE SUPERIOR CRAFTSMANSHIP.

"NEVER GIVE UP WITHOUT A FIGHT.

YUCK

"AND FOR AZULA, A NEW FRIEND. SHE WEARS THE LATEST FASHION FOR EARTH KINGDOM GIRLS."

IF UNCLE DOESN'T MAKE IT BACK FROM WAR, THEN DAD WOULD BE NEXT IN LINE TO BE FIRE LORD, WOULDN'T HE?

AZULA, WE DON'T SPEAK THAT WAY. IT WOULD BE AWFUL IF UNCLE IROH DIDN'T RETURN.

AND BESIDES, FIRE LORD AZULON IS A PICTURE OF HEALTH.

HOW WOULD YOU LIKE IT IF COUSIN LU TEN WANTED DAD TO DIE?

I STILL THINK OUR DAD WOULD MAKE A MUCH BETTER FIRE LORD THAN HIS ROYAL TEA-LOVING KOOKINESS.

FOOM

24

HYAH!

SWISH   SWISH

YOU'RE HOLDING THEM ALL WRONG.

AHH!

KEEP IN MIND, THESE ARE DUAL SWORDS.

TWO HALVES OF A SINGLE WEAPON. DON'T THINK OF THEM AS SEPARATE, BECAUSE THEY'RE NOT.

THEY'RE JUST TWO DIFFERENT PARTS OF THE SAME WHOLE.

SWISH

HAHA!

I THINK YOU'D REALLY LIKE MY BROTHER, SENSU. HE USED TO SHOW ME STUFF LIKE THIS ALL THE TIME.

HERE, THIS OUGHT TO GET YOU THROUGH A FEW MEALS.

RUMBLE
RUMBLE

RUMBLE RUMBLE

WHAT DO YOU THINK THEY WANT?

TROUBLE.

WHAT DO YOU WANT, GOW?

JUST THOUGHT SOMEONE OUGHT TO TELL YOU YOUR SON'S BATTALION GOT CAPTURED.

YOU BOYS HEAR WHAT THE FIRE NATION DID WITH THEIR LAST GROUP OF EARTH KINGDOM PRISONERS?

DRESSED 'EM UP IN FIRE NATION UNIFORMS AND PUT THEM ON THE FRONT LINE UNARMED, WAY I HEARD IT.

THEN THEY JUST WATCHED.

YOU WATCH YOUR MOUTH.

WHY BOTHER ROOTING AROUND IN THE MUD WITH THESE PIGS?

IROH HAS LOST HIS SON. YOUR COUSIN, LU TEN, DID NOT SURVIVE THE BATTLE.

WHAT'S GONNA HAPPEN TO MY BROTHER?

I'M GOING TO THE FRONT. I'M GOING TO FIND SENSU AND BRING HIM BACK.

WHEN MY DAD GOES, WILL YOU STAY?

NO. I NEED TO MOVE ON.

HERE, I WANT YOU TO HAVE THIS. READ THE INSCRIPTION.

"MADE IN EARTH KINGDOM."

THE OTHER ONE.

"NEVER GIVE UP WITHOUT A FIGHT."

HYAH!

AGGGHH!

You waste all your time playing with knives. You're not even good.

Put an apple on your head and we'll find out how good I am.

By the way, Uncle's coming home.

Does that mean we won the war?

No, it means Uncle's a quitter and a loser.

What are you talking about? Uncle's not a quitter.

Oh, yes, he is. He found out his son died and he just fell apart.

A real general would stay and burn Ba Sing Se to the ground.

NOT LOSE THE BATTLE AND COME HOME CRYING.

HOW DO YOU KNOW WHAT HE SHOULD DO? HE'S PROBABLY JUST SAD HIS ONLY KID IS GONE FOREVER.

YOUR FATHER HAS REQUESTED AN AUDIENCE WITH FIRE LORD AZULON.

BEST CLOTHES, HURRY UP.

"FIRE LORD AZULON." CAN'T YOU JUST CALL HIM GRANDFATHER? HE'S NOT EXACTLY THE POWERFUL FIRE LORD HE USED TO BE.

SOMEONE WILL PROBABLY END UP TAKING HIS PLACE SOON.

YOUNG LADY! NOT ANOTHER WORD!

WHAT IS WRONG WITH THAT CHILD?

AND HOW WAS IT GREAT-GRANDFATHER SOZIN MANAGED TO WIN THE BATTLE OF HAN TUI?

GREAT-GRANDFATHER WON BECAUSE...

BECAUSE EVEN THOUGH HIS ARMY WAS OUTNUMBERED, HE CLEVERLY CALCULATED HIS ADVANTAGES.

THE ENEMY WAS DOWNWIND, AND THERE WAS A DROUGHT. THEIR DEFENSES BURNED TO A CRISP IN MINUTES.

CORRECT, MY DEAR.

NOW, WOULD YOU SHOW GRANDFATHER THE NEW MOVES YOU DEMONSTRATED TO ME?

SHE'S A TRUE PRODIGY.

JUST LIKE HER GRANDFATHER FOR WHOM SHE'S NAMED.

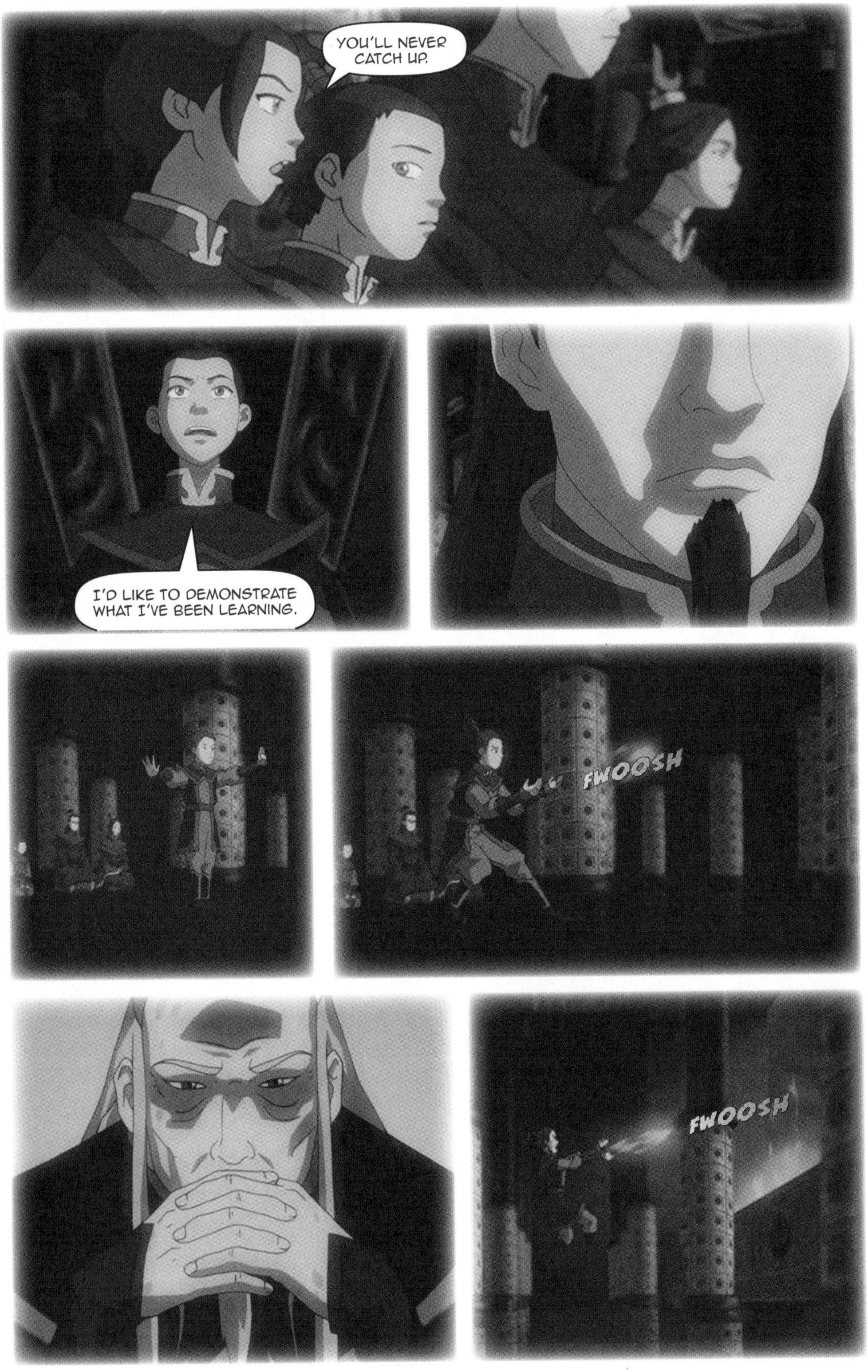
YOU'LL NEVER CATCH UP.
I'D LIKE TO DEMONSTRATE WHAT I'VE BEEN LEARNING.
FWOOSH
FWOOSH

OW!

BUMP

NO, I LOVED WATCHING YOU.

I FAILED...

THAT'S WHO YOU ARE, ZUKO. SOMEONE WHO KEEPS FIGHTING EVEN THOUGH IT'S HARD.

PRINCE OZAI, WHY ARE YOU WASTING MY TIME WITH THIS POMP? JUST TELL ME WHAT YOU WANT. EVERYONE ELSE, GO.

WHAT ARE YOU...

SHH!

FATHER, YOU MUST HAVE REALIZED, AS I HAVE...

THAT WITH LU TEN GONE, IROH'S BLOODLINE HAS ENDED.

AFTER HIS SON'S DEATH, MY BROTHER ABANDONED THE SIEGE AT BA SING SE. AND WHO KNOWS WHEN HE WILL RETURN HOME?

BUT I AM HERE, FATHER. AND MY CHILDREN ARE ALIVE.

SAY WHAT IT IS YOU WANT.

FATHER, REVOKE IROH'S BIRTHRIGHT. I AM YOUR HUMBLE SERVANT, HERE TO SERVE YOU AND OUR NATION. USE ME.

YOU DARE SUGGEST I BETRAY IROH? MY FIRSTBORN? DIRECTLY AFTER THE DEMISE OF HIS ONLY BELOVED SON?

I THINK IROH HAS SUFFERED ENOUGH. BUT YOU?

YOUR PUNISHMENT HAS SCARCELY BEGUN!

?

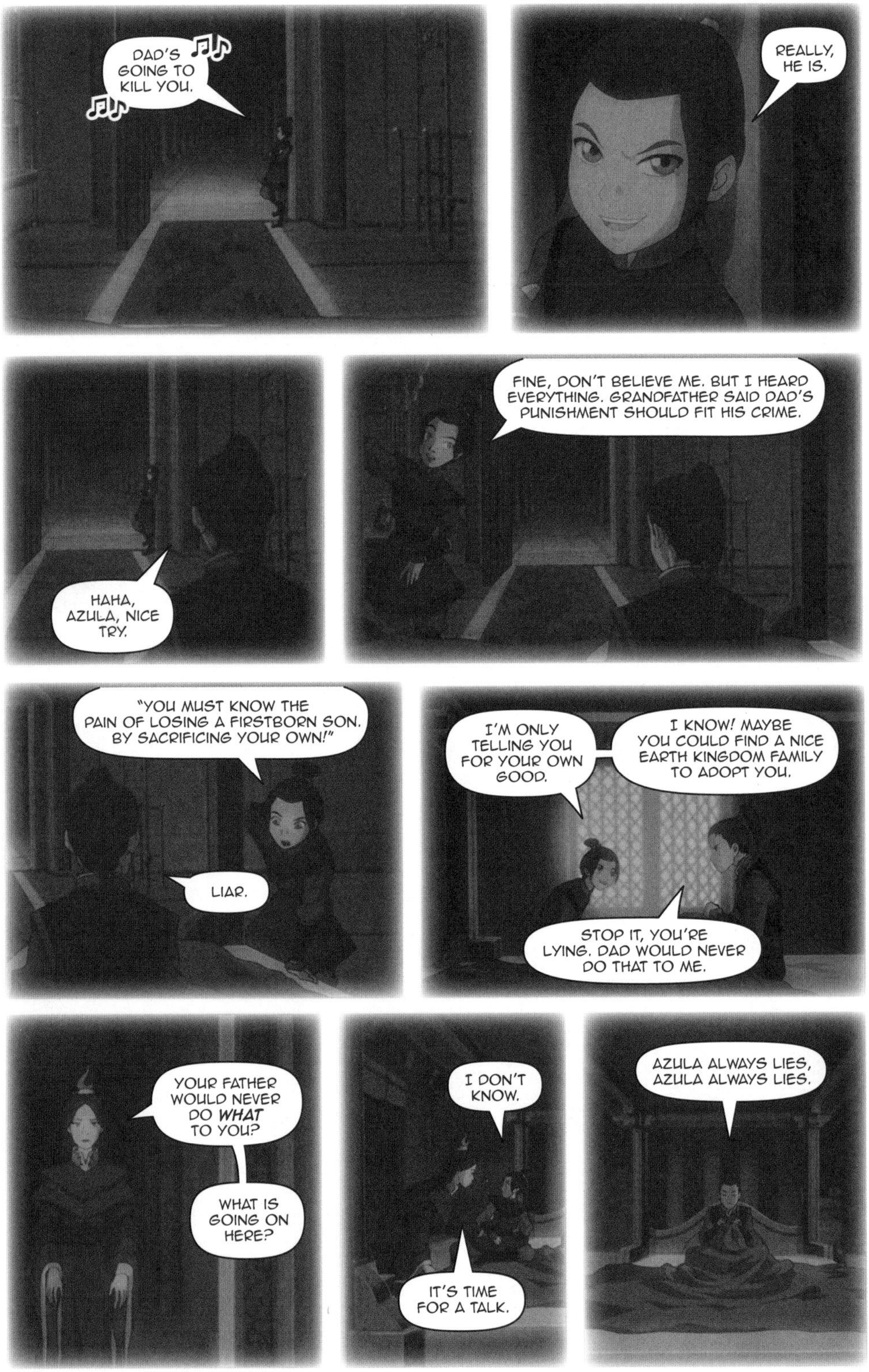
DAD'S GOING TO KILL YOU.
REALLY, HE IS.
HAHA, AZULA, NICE TRY.
FINE, DON'T BELIEVE ME. BUT I HEARD EVERYTHING. GRANDFATHER SAID DAD'S PUNISHMENT SHOULD FIT HIS CRIME.
"YOU MUST KNOW THE PAIN OF LOSING A FIRSTBORN SON. BY SACRIFICING YOUR OWN!"
LIAR.
I'M ONLY TELLING YOU FOR YOUR OWN GOOD.
I KNOW! MAYBE YOU COULD FIND A NICE EARTH KINGDOM FAMILY TO ADOPT YOU.
STOP IT, YOU'RE LYING. DAD WOULD NEVER DO THAT TO ME.
YOUR FATHER WOULD NEVER DO *WHAT* TO YOU?
WHAT IS GOING ON HERE?
I DON'T KNOW.
IT'S TIME FOR A TALK.
AZULA ALWAYS LIES, AZULA ALWAYS LIES.

AZULA ALWAYS LIES.

YOU HAVE TO HELP!

IT'S LEE. THE THUGS FROM TOWN CAME BACK AS SOON AS GANSU LEFT.

WHEN THEY ORDERED US TO GIVE THEM FOOD, LEE PULLED A KNIFE ON THEM!

I DON'T EVEN KNOW WHERE HE GOT A KNIFE!

THEN THEY TOOK HIM AWAY. THEY TOLD ME IF LEE'S OLD ENOUGH TO FIGHT, HE'S OLD ENOUGH TO JOIN THE ARMY!

I KNOW WE BARELY KNOW YOU, ÷SOB÷ BUT...

I'LL GET YOUR SON BACK.

HEY, THERE HE IS!

I TOLD YOU HE'D COME.

LET THE KID GO.

HAHAHA!

WHO DO YOU THINK YOU ARE? TELLING US WHAT TO DO?

IT DOESN'T MATTER WHO I AM. BUT I KNOW WHO YOU ARE. YOU'RE NOT SOLDIERS.

YOU'RE BULLIES. FREELOADERS ABUSING YOUR POWER.

MOSTLY OVER WOMEN AND KIDS. YOU DON'T WANT LEE IN YOUR ARMY.

YOU'RE SICK COWARDS MESSING WITH A FAMILY WHO'S ALREADY LOST ONE SON TO THE WAR.

ARE YOU GONNA LET THIS STRANGER STAND THERE AND INSULT YOU LIKE THIS?

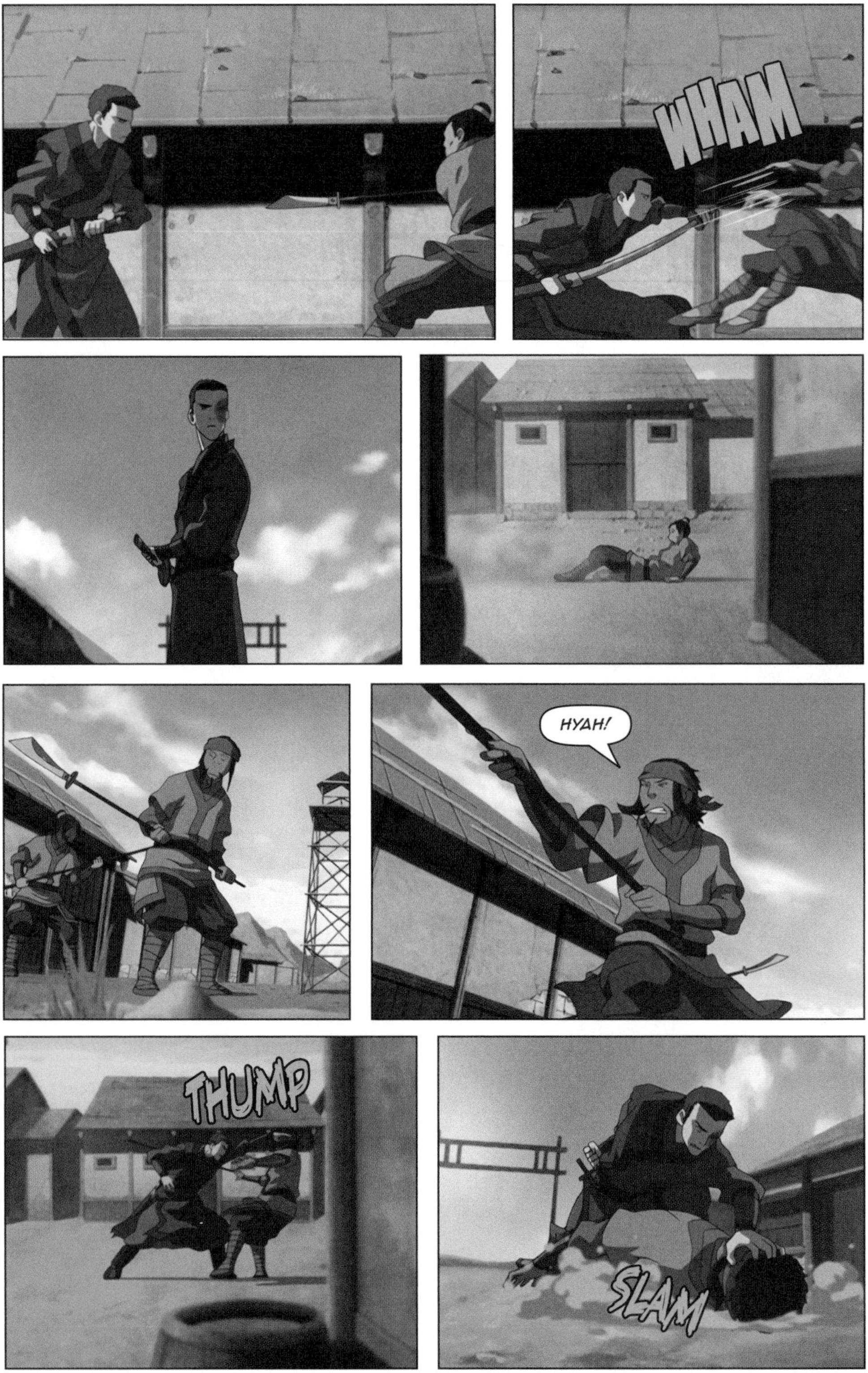
WHAM
HYAH!
THUMP
SLAM

AAAGHHH!

THWACK

HA-HA!

FWUMP

SMASH

WHUMP

GIVE HIM A LEFT!

IT'S NOT A FISTFIGHT.

HE'S GOT A LEFT SWORD, DON'T HE?

WHAM

LOOK OUT!

BEHIND YOU!

BOOM

AAAHHH!

WHAM

UGH!

MOM?

ZUKO, PLEASE, MY LOVE, LISTEN TO ME. EVERYTHING I'VE DONE, I'VE DONE TO PROTECT YOU.

REMEMBER THIS, ZUKO. NO MATTER HOW THINGS MAY SEEM TO CHANGE, NEVER FORGET WHO YOU ARE.

GET UP.

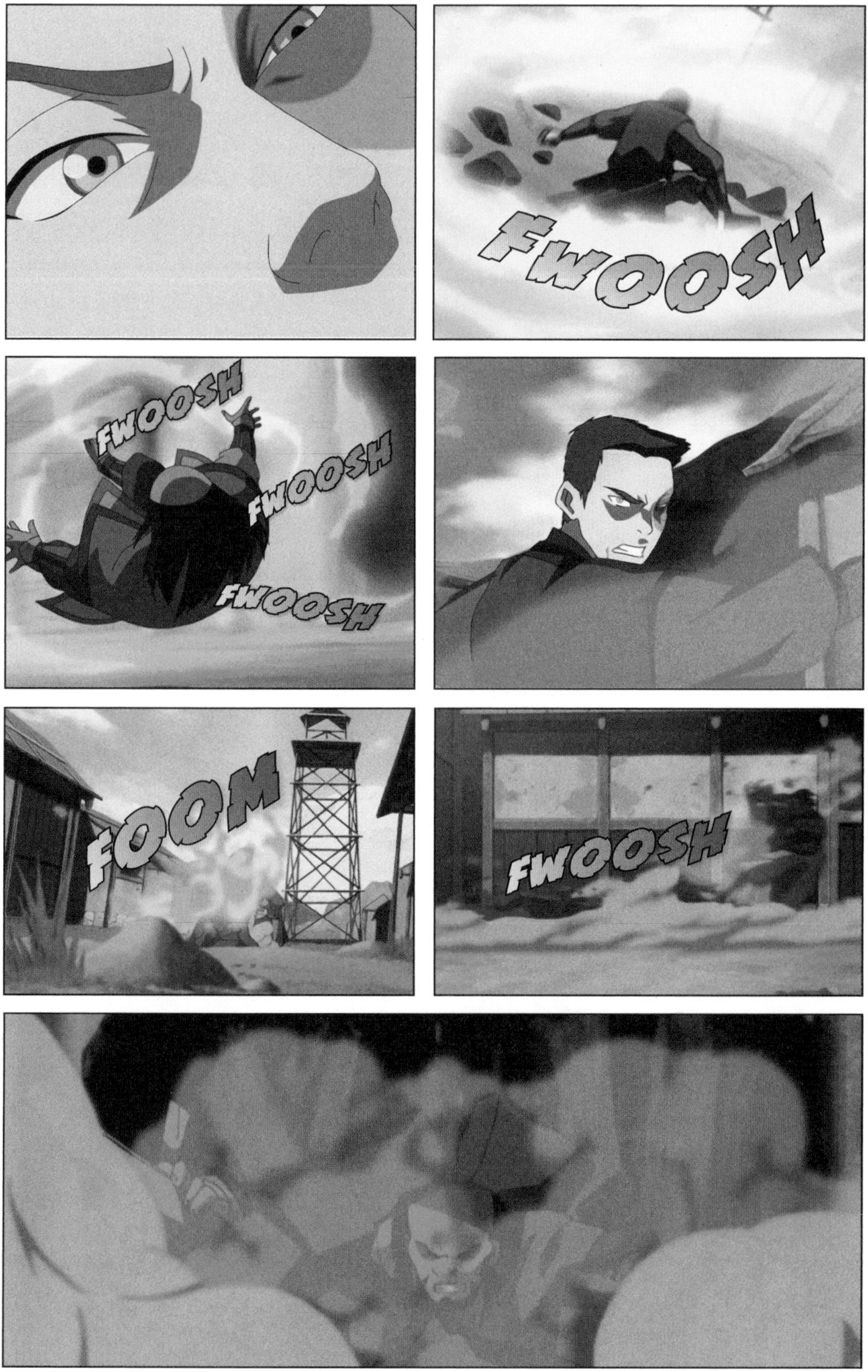
FWOOSH
FWOOSH
FWOOSH
FWOOSH
FOOM
FWOOSH

WHO...WHO ARE YOU?

MY NAME IS ZUKO. SON OF URSA AND FIRE LORD OZAI. PRINCE OF THE FIRE NATION AND HEIR TO THE THRONE!

LIAR! I HEARD OF YOU. YOU'RE NOT A PRINCE--YOU'RE AN OUTCAST!

HIS OWN FATHER BURNED AND DISOWNED HIM!

NOT A STEP CLOSER.

IT'S YOURS, YOU SHOULD HAVE IT.

NO, I HATE YOU.

MOM?

MOM! MOM!

WHERE'S MOM?

NO ONE KNOWS.

OH, AND LAST NIGHT, GRANDPA PASSED AWAY.

NOT FUNNY, AZULA. YOU'RE SICK. AND I WANT MY KNIFE BACK, NOW.

WHO'S GOING TO MAKE ME? MOM?

WHERE IS SHE?

AZULON, FIRE LORD TO OUR NATION FOR TWENTY-THREE YEARS, YOU WERE OUR FEARLESS LEADER IN THE BATTLE OF GARSAI. OUR MATCHLESS CONQUEROR OF THE HU XIN PROVINCES.

YOU WERE FATHER OF IROH. FATHER OF OZAI. HUSBAND OF ILAH, NOW PASSED.

GRANDFATHER OF LU TEN, NOW PASSED. GRANDFATHER OF ZUKO AND AZULA. WE LAY YOU TO REST.

AS WAS YOUR DYING WISH, YOU ARE NOW SUCCEEDED BY YOUR SECOND SON.

HAIL FIRE
LORD OZAI!

HAIL FIRE
LORD OZAI!

DAYS LATER...

BOOM

UGH!

OHH!

THAT REALLY HURT MY TAILBONE.

ALL RIGHT. YOU'VE CAUGHT UP WITH ME. NOW, WHO ARE YOU, AND WHAT DO YOU WANT?

YOU MEAN, YOU HAVEN'T GUESSED? YOU DON'T SEE THE FAMILY RESEMBLANCE?

HERE'S A HINT...

I MUST FIND THE AVATAR TO RESTORE MY HONOR.

IT'S OKAY. YOU CAN LAUGH. IT'S FUNNY.

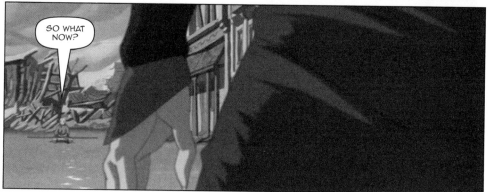

SO WHAT NOW?

NOW? NOW IT'S OVER.

YOU'RE TIRED, AND YOU HAVE NO PLACE TO GO. YOU CAN RUN, BUT I'LL CATCH YOU.

I'M NOT RUNNING.

HERE IS YOUR TEA.

YOU SEEM A LITTLE TOO YOUNG TO BE TRAVELING ALONE.

YOU SEEM A LITTLE TOO OLD.

HAHA! PERHAPS I AM.

I KNOW WHAT YOU'RE THINKING. I LOOK LIKE I CAN'T HANDLE BEING BY MYSELF.

I WASN'T THINKING THAT.

YOU WOULDN'T LET ME POUR MY OWN CUP OF TEA.

I POURED YOUR TEA BECAUSE I WANTED TO AND FOR NO OTHER REASON.

PEOPLE SEE ME AND THINK I'M WEAK.

THEY WANT TO TAKE CARE OF ME, BUT I CAN TAKE CARE OF MYSELF BY MYSELF.

YOU SOUND LIKE MY NEPHEW, ALWAYS THINKING YOU NEED TO DO THINGS ON YOUR OWN WITHOUT ANYONE'S SUPPORT.

THERE IS NOTHING WRONG WITH LETTING PEOPLE WHO LOVE YOU HELP YOU.

NOT THAT I LOVE YOU. WELL, I JUST MET YOU.

HEE-HEE

SO WHERE IS YOUR NEPHEW?

I'VE BEEN TRACKING HIM, ACTUALLY.

IS HE LOST?

YES, A LITTLE BIT.

HIS LIFE HAS RECENTLY CHANGED, AND HE'S GOING THROUGH VERY DIFFICULT TIMES.

HE'S TRYING TO FIGURE OUT WHO HE IS, AND HE WENT AWAY.

SO NOW YOU'RE FOLLOWING HIM.

I KNOW HE DOESN'T WANT ME AROUND RIGHT NOW, BUT IF HE NEEDS ME, I'LL BE THERE.

YOUR NEPHEW IS VERY LUCKY, EVEN IF HE DOESN'T KNOW IT.

THANK YOU.

MY PLEASURE. SHARING TEA WITH A FASCINATING STRANGER IS ONE OF LIFE'S TRUE DELIGHTS.

I'M GLAD.

NO. THANK YOU FOR WHAT YOU SAID. IT HELPED ME.

OH, AND ABOUT YOUR NEPHEW. MAYBE YOU SHOULD TELL HIM THAT YOU NEED HIM, TOO.

60

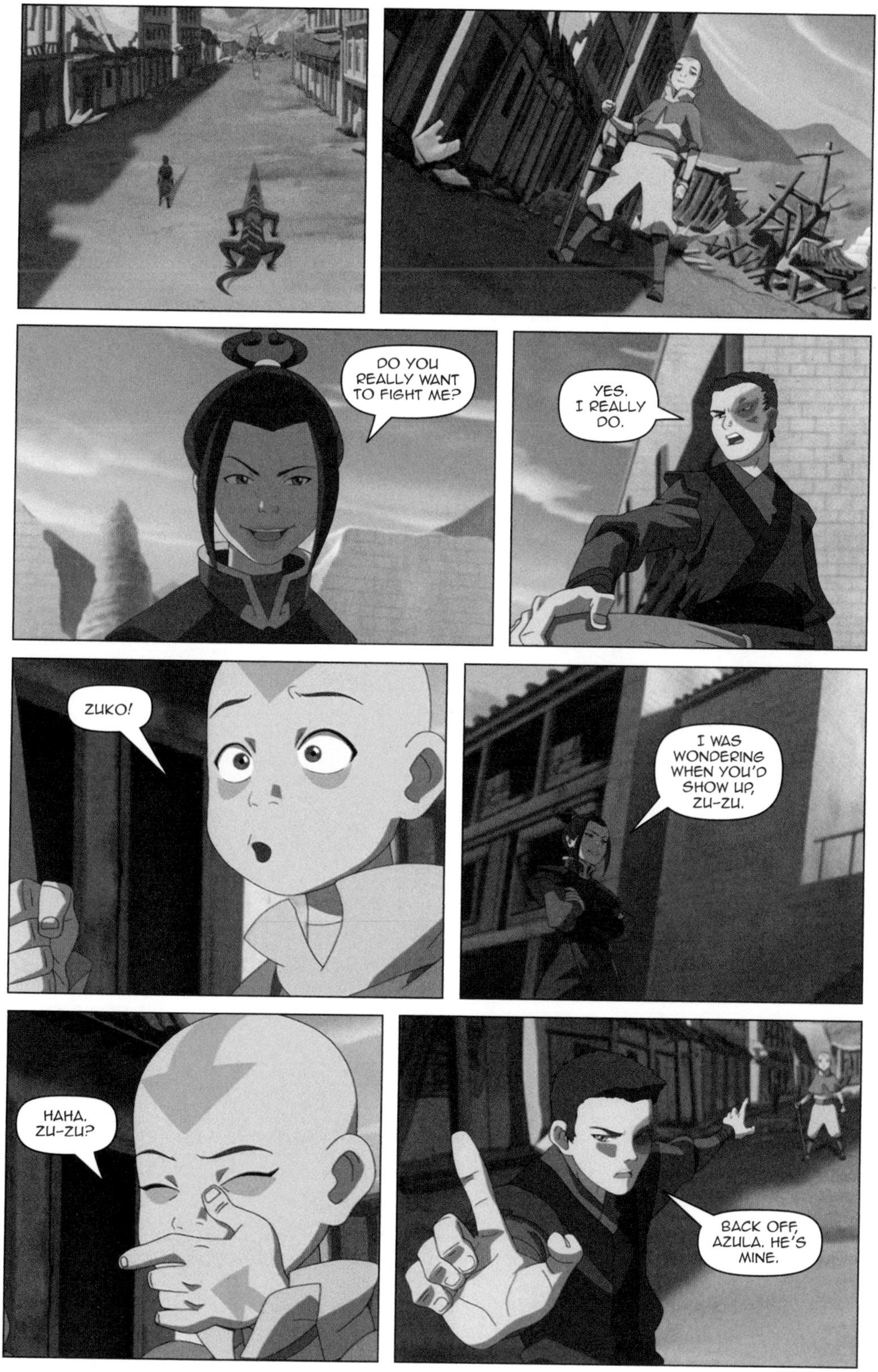
DO YOU REALLY WANT TO FIGHT ME?
YES. I REALLY DO.
ZUKO!
I WAS WONDERING WHEN YOU'D SHOW UP, ZU-ZU.
HAHA. ZU-ZU?
BACK OFF, AZULA. HE'S MINE.

I'M NOT GOING ANYWHERE.

FSHOOM

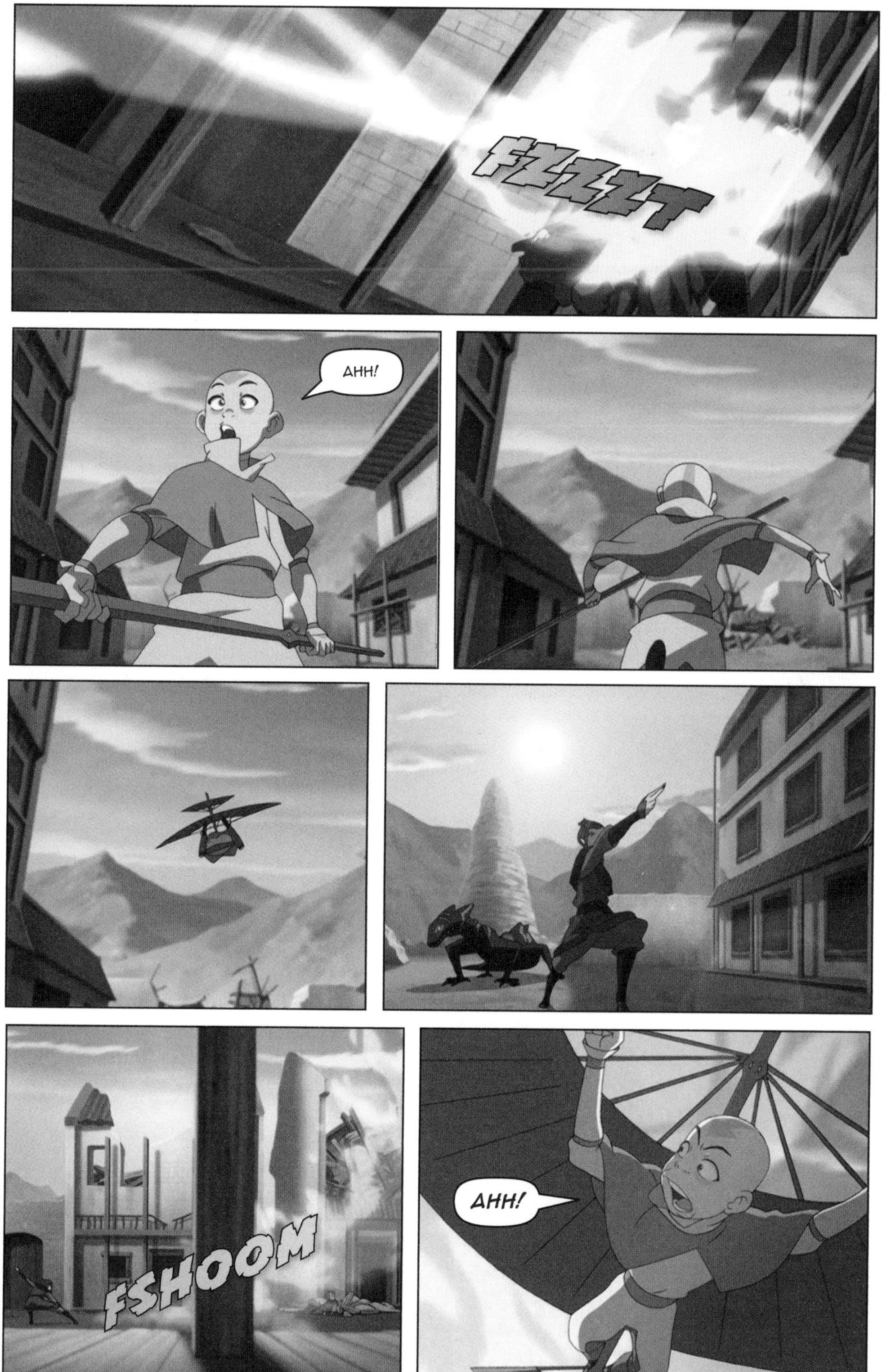
FZZZZT
AHH!
FSHOOM
AHH!

FOOM

FOOM
FOOM

AHHH!

FSHOOM

FSHOOM

64

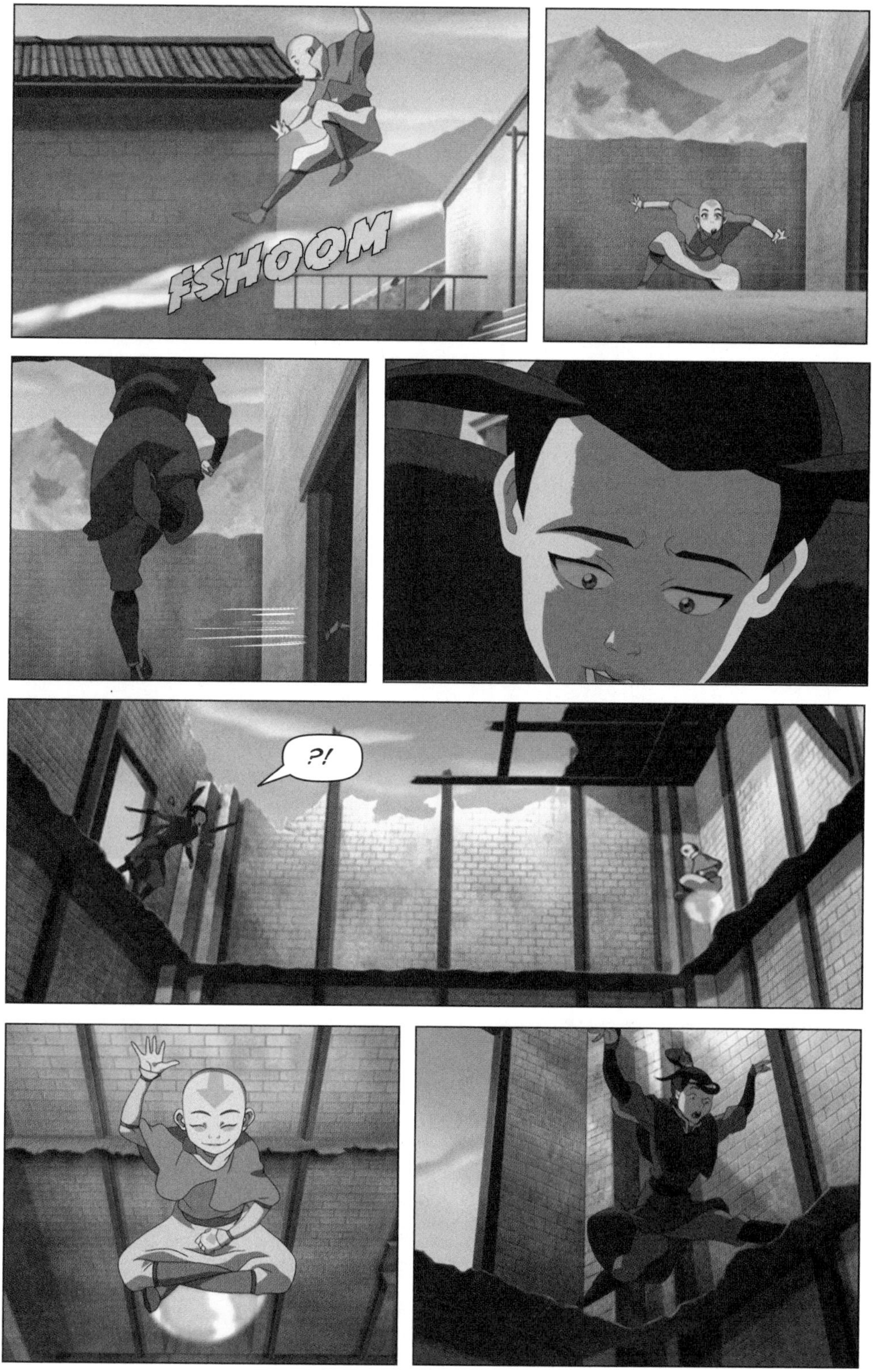
FSHOOM
?!

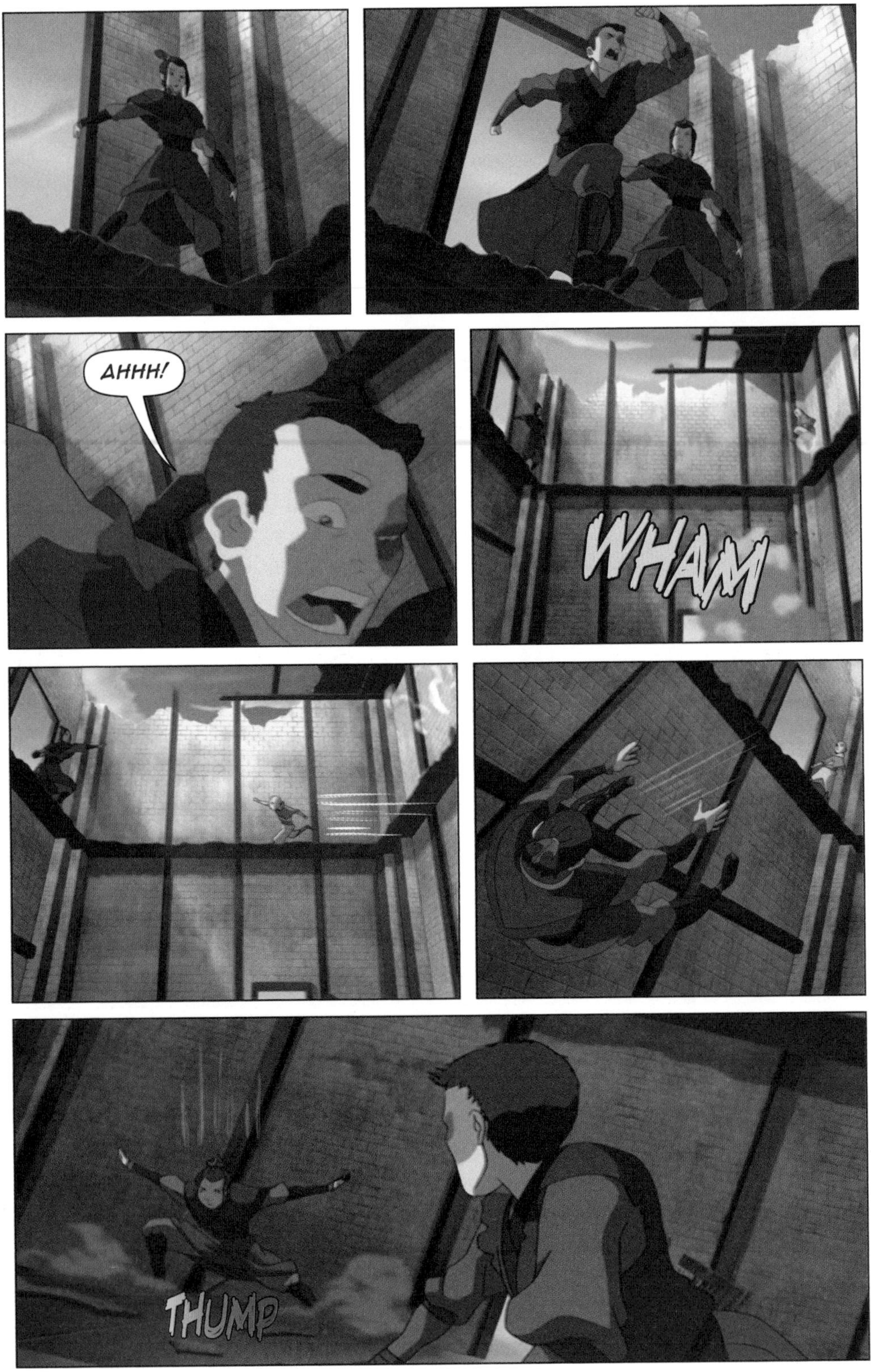
AHHH!
WHAM
THUMP

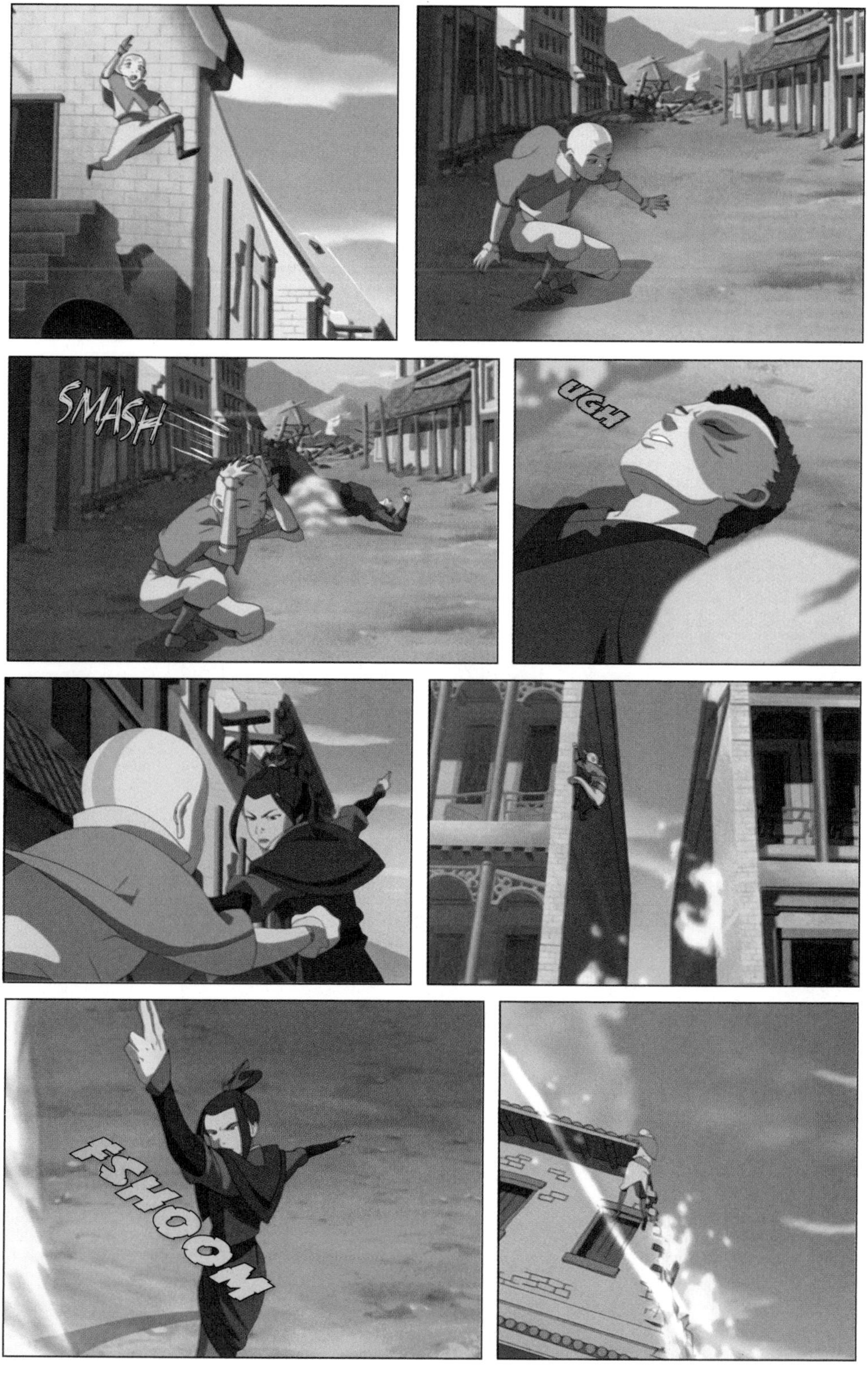
SMASH
UGH
FSHOOM

AHHH!

UGH!

FLOOOOSHHH

KATARA!

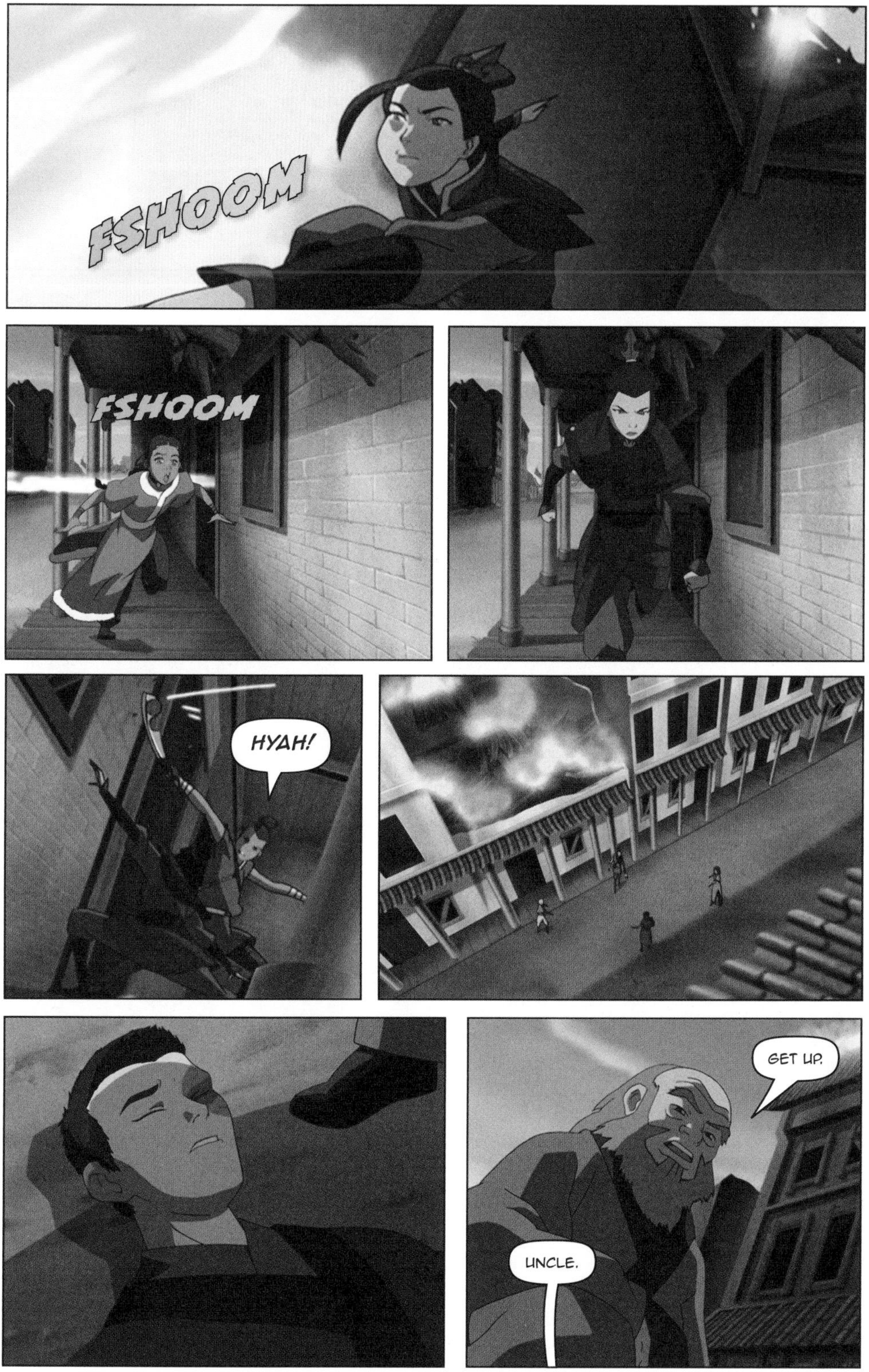
FSHOOM
FSHOOM
HYAH!
GET UP.
UNCLE.

SLAM

I THOUGHT YOU GUYS COULD USE A LITTLE HELP.

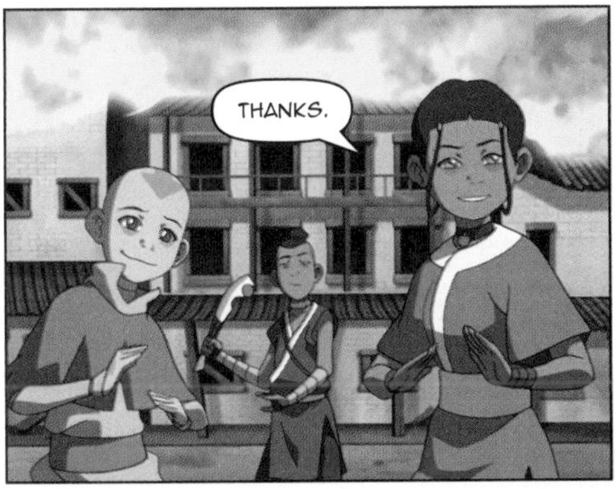
THANKS.
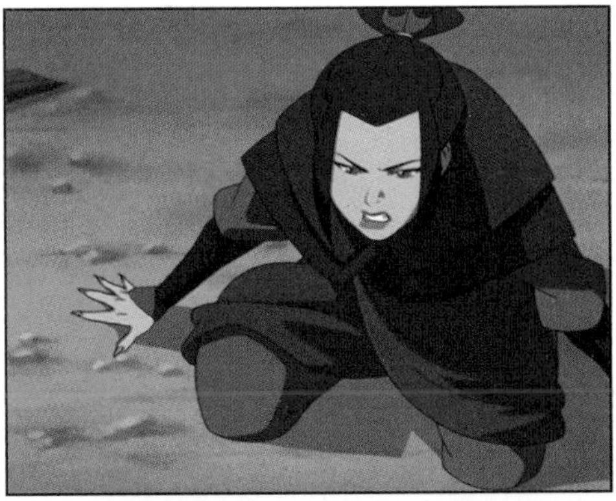
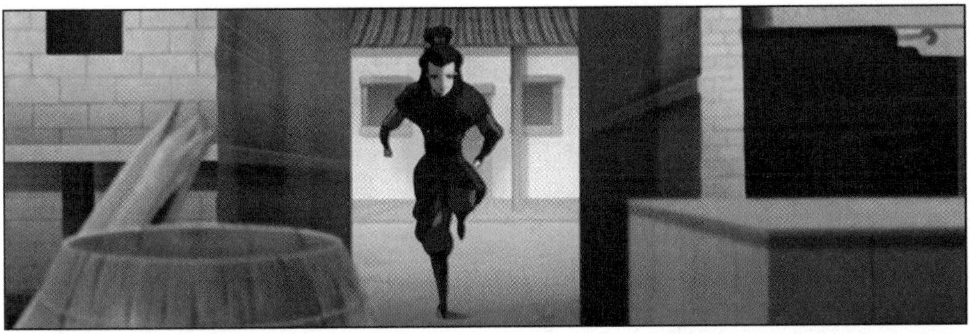
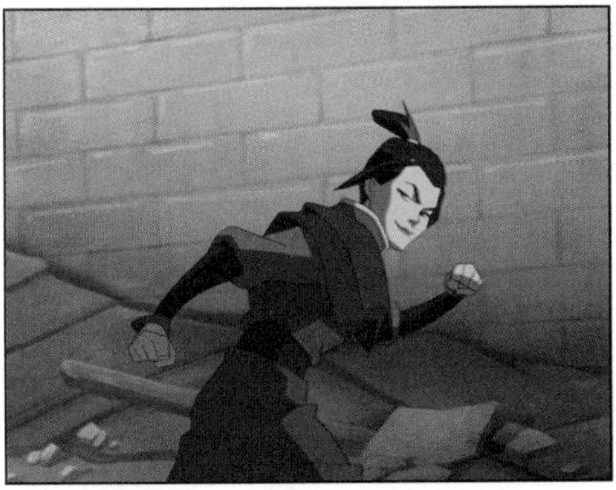
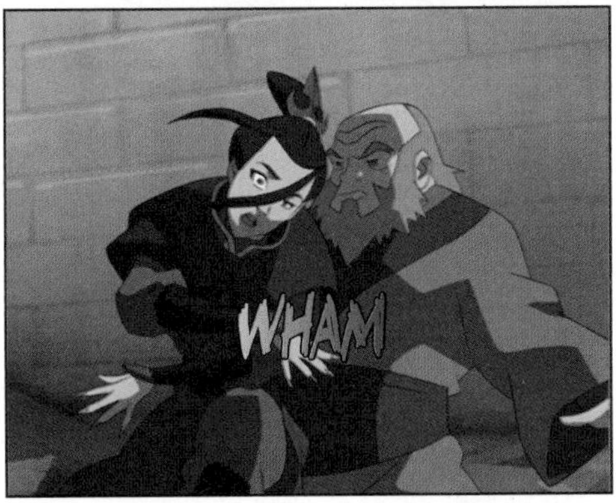
WHAM
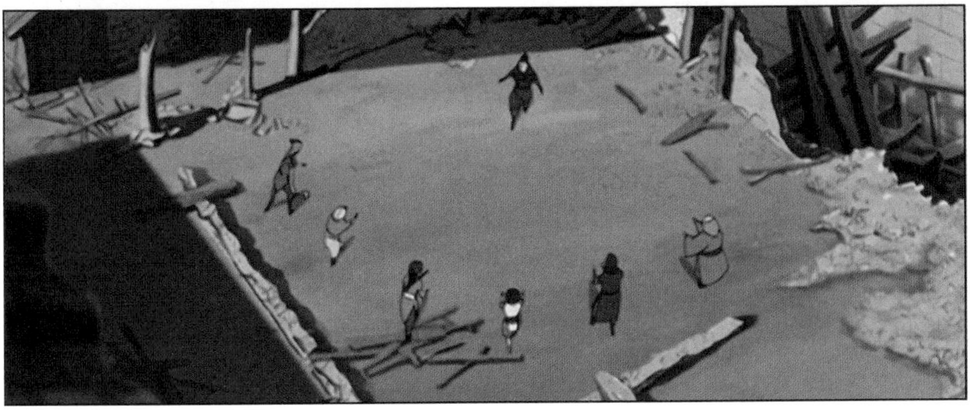

WELL, LOOK AT THIS. ENEMIES AND TRAITORS ALL WORKING TOGETHER.

I'M DONE. I KNOW WHEN I'M BEATEN. YOU GOT ME.

A PRINCESS SURRENDERS WITH HONOR.

FSHOOM

AHHH!

ZZZT

AHHH!

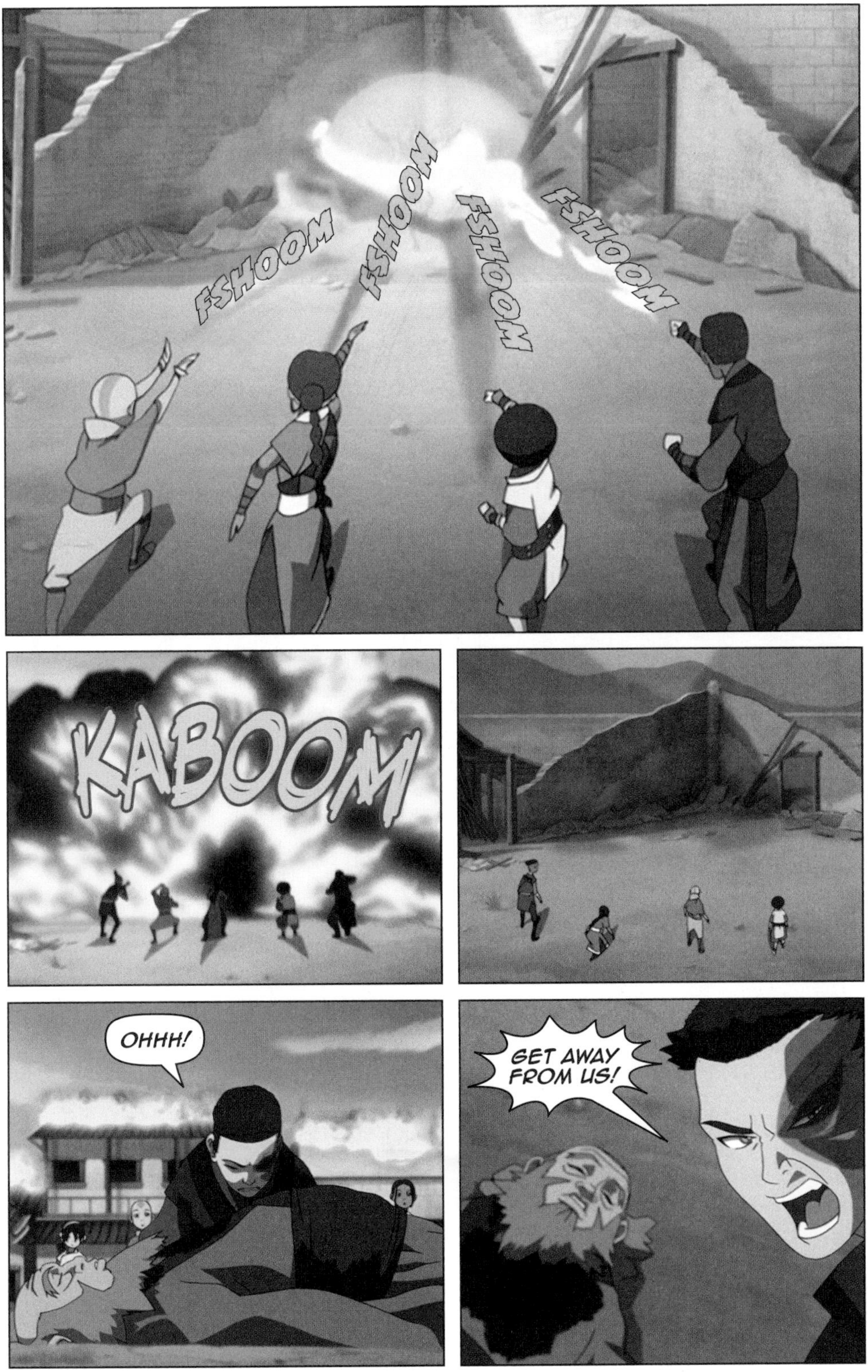
FSHOOM
FSHOOM
FSHOOM
FSHOOM
KABOOM
OHHH!
GET AWAY FROM US!

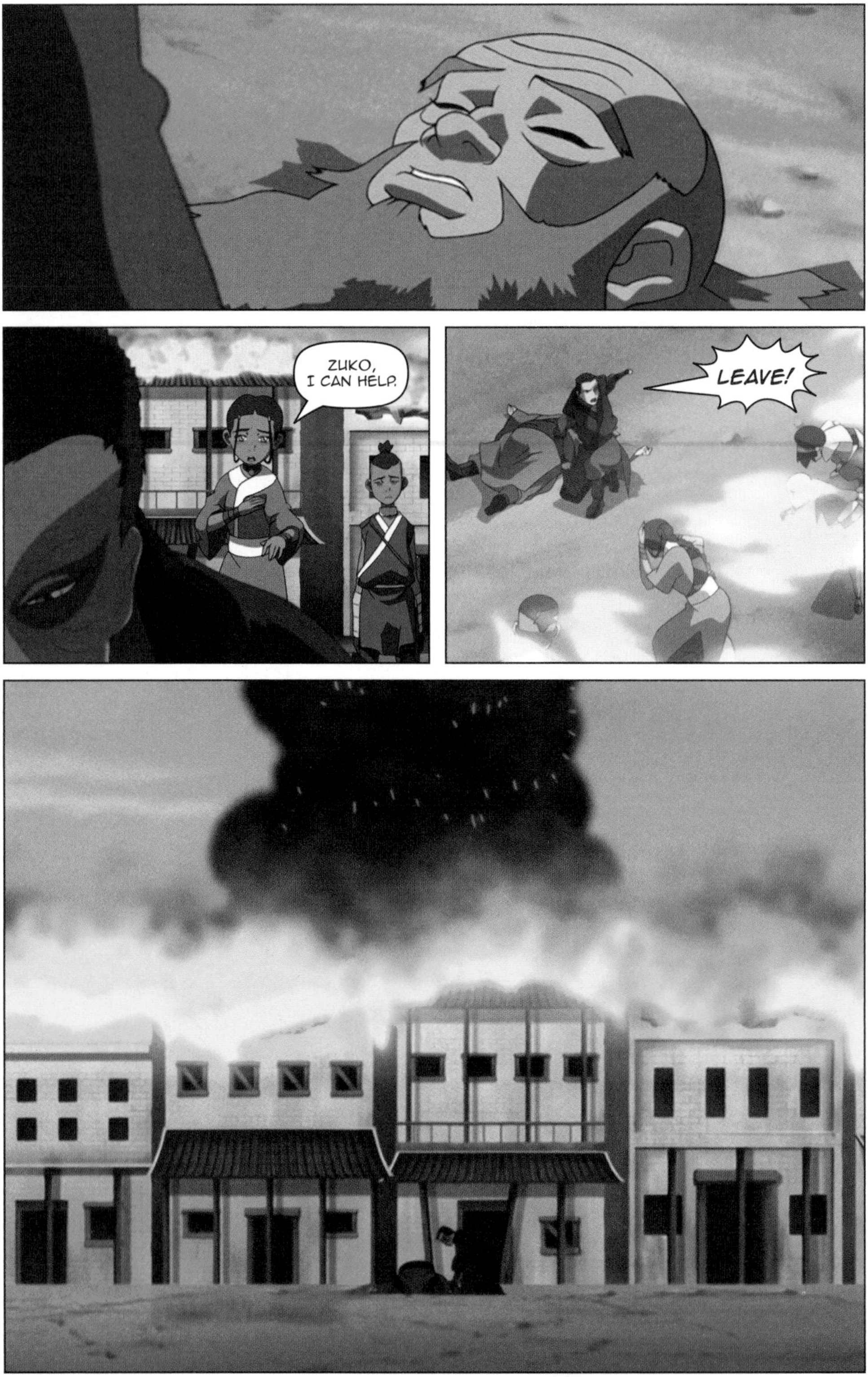
ZUKO, I CAN HELP.
LEAVE!

LATER...

UNCLE. YOU WERE UNCONSCIOUS.

AZULA DID THIS TO YOU.

IT WAS A SURPRISE ATTACK.

SOMEHOW THAT'S NOT SO SURPRISING.

I HOPE I MADE IT THE WAY YOU LIKE IT.

MMM. GOOD.

THAT WAS VERY, UM, BRACING.

"YOU MUST LET GO OF YOUR FEELINGS OF SHAME IF YOU WANT YOUR ANGER TO GO AWAY. PRIDE IS NOT THE OPPOSITE OF SHAME, BUT ITS SOURCE. TRUE HUMILITY IS THE ONLY ANTIDOTE TO SHAME."
--UNCLE IROH

CREDITS

AVATAR DAY

WRITTEN BY JOHN O'BRYAN

HEAD WRITER
AARON EHASZ

DIRECTED BY LAUREN MACMULLAN

CO-EXECUTIVE PRODUCER
AARON EHASZ

ZUKO ALONE

WRITTEN BY ELIZABETH WELCH EHASZ

HEAD WRITER
AARON EHASZ

DIRECTED BY LAUREN MACMULLAN

CO-EXECUTIVE PRODUCER
AARON EHASZ

THE CHASE

WRITTEN BY JOSHUA HAMILTON

HEAD WRITER
AARON EHASZ

DIRECTED BY GIANCARLO VOLPE

CO-EXECUTIVE PRODUCER
AARON EHASZ

BITTER WORK

WRITTEN BY AARON EHASZ

HEAD WRITER
AARON EHASZ

DIRECTED BY ETHAN SPAULDING

CO-EXECUTIVE PRODUCER
AARON EHASZ

nickelodeon

降世神通
AVATAR
THE LAST AIRBENDER

EXECUTIVE PRODUCERS: MICHAEL DANTE DiMARTINO & BRYAN KONIETZKO